ON WINGS THE WIND

BY RUTH & LARRY BRADFORD
ILLUSTRATED BY ANNABEL MONTGOMERY

To order additional copies of this book, contact:
Xlibris
1-888-795-4274
www.Xlibris.com
Orders@Xlibris.com

Scripture quotations marked KJV are from the Holy Bible, King
James Version (Authorized Version). First published in 1611.
Quoted from the KJV Classic Reference Bible, Copyright © 1983
by The Zondervan Corporation.

ISBN: Softcover   978-1-7960-6334-9
        EBook   978-1-7960-6333-2

Print information available on the last page

Rev. date: 10/03/2019

ON WINGS OF THE WIND
By Ruth and Larry Bradford
Illustrated by Annabel Montgomery

<u>Psalm 104:3</u> Who layeth the beams of his chambers in the waters: who maketh the clouds his chariot: who walketh upon the wings of the wind.

The whirling winds brought a wicked cold winter early. The deep darkness began the very day Grandpa Bell smiled then sighed, "Lord, I'm ready." He closed his eyes and breathed his last breath on earth. Grandpa Bell was carried on the wings of the wind straight to Heaven.

Randolph Raven flapped onto the smooth leafless branch where Hoover the great horned owl sat chuckling to himself and ruffling his grayish-brown and white feathers.

"Sad times, Hoover, sad times." Randolph clacked his beak.

"Hungry times, Randolph, hungry times." The owl lifted off the branch and soared silently over the dry corn field, looking more like a ghost than a bird.

****

An old red Chevy pickup bounced up the rutty dirt road. Harper Bell and his two girls, eleven-year old Lucy, and five-year old Charlotte sang "I'm a Little Piece of Tin. Nobody knows where I have been. Got four wheels and a running board. I'm a Ford, a Ford, a Ford. Bump, bump, rattle, rattle." Then they started the second verse making each word start with 'b.' The bouncing made their voices bounce. "Bi'm a bittle biece of bin. Bobody bows bere bi bave been. Bot bour beels and a bunning board. Bi'm a bord, a bord, a bord. Bump, bump, battle, battle." All three laughed out loud!

Harper was tall and thin with dark straight hair. Sadness had etched deep wrinkles into his brow, but smile wrinkles also creased around his eyes and lips.

Harper stopped in front of the big dark house.

"Now girls, remember what I said, Grandpa Bell isn't here. He went to be with Jesus. But he wanted us to have his farm. So we must fix it up with joy!"

"Of course, Dad!" the girls agreed.

Big dark clouds swallowed the setting sun. Darkness dropped like a curtain. A streak of lightning split the clouds, followed by a long drumroll of thunder.

Charlotte pulled at her father's blue windbreaker. "Daddy…"

"Girls, we have to get these boxes into the house before it starts raining or snowing," he said.

"Daddy!" Charlotte tugged so hard on his jacket he almost dropped the big box he was holding.

"Look!" She pointed at two birds sitting together on a branch.

"Well, now that is a strange welcoming committee! I've never seen a great horned owl and a raven socializing."

Harper greeted the two large birds. "Glad to meet you, feathered friends. I am Harper Bell, and these are my two daughters, Lucy and Charlotte. Thank you for welcoming us into your neighborhood."

****

Five cottontail rabbits were huddled in the lean-to, attached to the back of the once elegant house. They felt safe because the only way in or out was through a small hole, just big enough for each bunny to wiggle through. The big door was closed tight.

"We need a plan," Bopper, the biggest bunny said.

"A plan? Why?" chorused the three small bunnies: Fifi, Foo-Foo, and Fluffy.

"The coyotes have gotten bolder since Grandpa Bell went to heaven, especially that big one they call Buster. If he sees us out…well, let's just say someone will have dinner!" Bopper, the oldest bunny explained.

"Oh, dear," Fifi said.

"Dinner?" Foo-Foo said.

"Oh, no!" Fluffy said.

"Yeah, we would be the dinner!" Fred, the middle-sized bunny said sadly. He covered his nose with his paw.

"Yeah!" came a wheezy sound from just outside the lean-too.

"H…h…h!" Fifi drew in a big breath, her eyes wide with fear.

"Ah, it's just the wind," Fred said, trying to sound brave.

"Okay, if we don't have a plan we will starve to death," Bopper said. His voice was lower. "I'm the biggest and baddest, so I will collect food …from the old garden… if I can find some." His voice trailed off as he looked at each bunny. "The corn is gone in the corn patch. But I think I can still dig up a few old carrots and maybe a beet or turnip."

"I will keep an eye out for the enemy," Fred said. "I'm the best at hiding. And then when you dig up some food, I'll carry it really fast here to the lean-to!"

"Yes, you are fast, Fred." Bopper patted his little brother's head."Fluffy, Foo-Foo, and Fifi, you act as look-outs. If you see anything strange, meaning the nasty coyotes, thump really loud! Fred, hide under the bush by the old garden gate. I will pass you the food and you run like crazy. Pass it to the girls. Then hightail it back for the next load…if I can find more."

"Yes, sir. You can count on me!"

"Heh, heh, heh," chuckled the coyote.

"Shhh," Bopper said.

"What was that?" Fred whispered. "Not the wind."

Bopper looked. He sniffed. His ears twitched this way and that way. But he didn't look up.

Fred looked. He sniffed. His ears twitched this way and that way. But he didn't look up.

The three bunny girls looked. They sniffed and whimpered quietly. But they didn't look up.

"We will rest tonight. Bopper and his buddies will howl and prowl all night. Then at first light, when they are all sleepy, we will carry out our plan."

"Heh, heh, heh! Yeah, their plan will work just fine," Buster chuckled, "For me!" He slunk away to join his gang.

****

The sun was just peeking over the eastern hills, painting the clouds deep pink and gold. Bopper had found three shriveled up carrots and one tough beet.

It was Fred's first trip. He carried the three small carrots clamped firmly in his jaws. He watched. He ran. He stopped. He sniffed the air. He made one high spy-jump.

Unfortunately, that spy-jump was what caught Buster's attention.

"Wake up, you lazy bums!" Buster howled then coughed. After all, it had been a beautiful night for howling at the full moon, even though it only played peek-a-boo through the thick clouds a few times during the night. They hadn't found much to eat except for an unlucky old gopher. They were tired and ready for their morning snooze. "Remember what I said. You guys get the biggest rabbit in the old garden! I'll go after the medium-sized one, because he's fast, and I'm…well… I'm Buster! I'm the best!"

Sure enough, Bopper was just digging up a wrinkly turnip, when the coyote brothers surrounded him. His head went up just as he heard the half-howl, half-cough. But he kept digging until too late.

Two of the coyote brothers moved in on Bopper. One grabbed the big rabbit by the skin of his back. Bopper squealed and kicked hard. His sharp hind claws caught the coyote, 'bam!' Right on his black nose!

"Hey! You're supposed to be a wimpy little bunny!" The coyote dropped Bopper and rubbed his nose with his paw.

Bopper tried to run after Fred toward the lean-to, but his back felt like fire, and he felt a wetness oozing from the bite in his back. He felt so weak. Bopper thought, "Maybe I should just be dinner?"

But he knew he couldn't give up. He had to think of his family. He made himself pull his strong hind legs up, ready for another kick.

The coyote brothers moved in for the kill.

Buster was almost on top of Fred. Then young bunny made an amazing jump forward. He zigged and zagged until he got to the lean-to. He wriggled through the hole, just as Buster grabbed his cottony tail.

Lucky for Fred, all Buster got was a mouthful of white fuzzy fur.

What the coyotes didn't see were two shadows above them growing larger and larger by the second. By the time they felt the talons and beaks of Hoover and Randolph, their idea of a meal totally changed to the hope of escaping, with their ears, noses, and eyes still in working order.

"Dad! Dad!" Charlotte and Lucy came running into the house. The girls carried a cardboard box between them.

"Just a minute, girls." Harper was talking on his cell phone. "Yes, sir. I am sure we can be ready to board your horses. Yes, sir, by the end of the month."

"Well, my dear girls, we are in business for boarding and doctoring animals," he said. "Now what do you have in that box?"

"Look, Papa! Here is our first patient. This bunny got hurt by something," Lucy said. "Maybe that owl or raven!"

"No! It was not the owl or the raven!" Charlotte glared at Lucy. "Can we save him, Dad?" She looked up at Harper with tears in her eyes.

"Let's see," he said. He put on plastic gloves. Then he knelt by the box. "He is still breathing, but we need to see where he is bleeding."

"Ohhh," the rabbit moaned.

"He says, it was bad coyotes. One bit his back," Charlotte said. She turned and glared at Lucy. "See! I told you it wasn't Hoover or Randolph!"

"You're right, Charlotte. I know you can understand the animals, like I used to when I was young," Lucy said, matter-of-factly. "Now, I am learning to doctor from you, Father. I think I can stitch his cuts." Her brown pony tail bobbed up and down as she worked over the scared little rabbit.

"I am sure you can, Lucy. You girls are so amazing," Harper said.

After she stitched and disinfected the wounds, Harper helped Lucy give the bunny a shot of antibiotic to avoid infection.

"Hmmmm," Bopper the bunny hummed.

Charlotte said quietly, "His name is Bopper, and he says he feels much better, thank you."

Darkness deepened as if a huge shadow covered the land. The mountains disappeared into the gloom.

"Okay, my darling girls. What's for lunch?" Harper asked. He hung his coat on a hook. "It looks like a storm is moving in. We'd better get a fire started and eat something. Then we need to fasten the shutters over the windows, and make sure the barn is closed up tight."

"PB & J!" Charlotte smiled hopefully.

"Maybe PB &J, after you eat my good, hot chicken soup. It has lots of veggies," Lucy said firmly. She had become quite the cook since their mother had died two years ago, after a long struggle with cancer.

"It smells delicious. Dish it up," Harper said. "I'm hungry."

"Dear Jesus, thank You for this soup. And thank You for the animals that we can help. Amen." Charlotte quickly added, "And for PB & J!"

"Ha ha! That's my Charlotte!" Harper laughed.

"Humph!" Lucy frowned, but then she laughed, too.

****

Big wet snowflakes began to tumble from the clouds. The wind whipped the flakes sideways. It became a blizzard…a white-out.

Twelve-year old, dark-haired, Brent Swenson was tired from chopping and stacking wood. He had begun working odd jobs since the bakery burned down. His mother was a master baker. But when the bakery burned, she no longer had a job. And their apartment over the bakery was gone, too, along with most of their belongings. Now they were staying in a small hotel room, but could only barely pay the rent and buy food with the money Brent brought home.

Brent yelled at God, "Why do bad things happen to good people? My mama loves You and tells me that everything will work out for good. So why did you let that fire burn everything?" Tears stung his eyes.

The wind and snow chilled him to his bones. He pulled his faded gray hoodie around him, but it didn't help much.

He put one foot in front of the other, thinking the hotel was just ahead through the trees. He hadn't paid attention to the sky, until the snow surrounded him, and the wind confused his sense of direction.

"Daddy, come to the barn, please!" Charlotte took Harper's hand. "Lucy needs your help with our newest patient."

"It's getting late and the snow is getting deep. What does she need help with?" Harper asked, as he pulled on his coat and red-and-black plaid cap with ear flaps.

Charlotte had her red wool cap over her brown curls. Her cheeks were pink with excitement. "It's an owl, Daddy, a biiiiig owl! Remember the owl and the raven that met us when we first came? Randolph Raven brought Hoover Owl to the loft in the barn."

"Oh!" Harper dug some long leather gloves out of the storage box. Together, father and daughter slogged through the fiercely blowing snow to the barn.

The big owl's wing hung at a crooked angle and several long flight feathers were missing. His eyes glowed in the dim light of the barn.

"I saw about ten crows in a murder. That's what people call a group of crows…" Randolph started.

"I know, that's what those murderous birds are!" Hoover interrupted angrily.

"Well, anyway, I saw them attacking you, Hoover. I tried to talk to them, but, well…their black hearts weren't listening," Randolph said.

"I know. I know. They have been after me since last spring. Two of their brothers were after our three chicks. Those chicks screamed for food day and night, night and day. Maizy, that's my wife, and I had to hunt for food non-stop. Those two crow brothers were the meanest. They knocked little George right out of the nest." Hoover ruffled his feathers at the memory.

"Hooooo…Owww!" A sharp pain shot through his hurt wing. He lost his balance and fell backward onto the barn floor below. Fortunately he landed on a pile of hay.

"Oooof."

"Hoover! Hoover! Are you dead?" Randolph dove to his side.

"Oooooo. I wish," Hoover moaned.

"So what happened to those two mean crows? And was George okay?"

"George is fine. He's living in the foothills, now. But those two crows won't bother anybody, anymore. All that was left of them was a few black wing feathers."

****

Charlotte and Harper came through the big barn door, followed by a blast of wind and snow. Harper shoved the door closed.

"So where is this injured owl?" he asked.

"He was up in the loft with Randolph, but he fell onto that pile of hay," Lucy said. She was busy making a tiny splint for a roadrunner, whose delicate leg had broken.

Charlotte approached close, but not too close, to the two birds. "What happened?" she asked.

She listened carefully to the conversation of hisses, coos, whistles, and clacking of beaks between Randolph and poor Hoover, who lay flat on his back, so limp, you might have thought he was dead.

"Don't worry," Charlotte said sweetly to the two big birds. "Hoover, my daddy is here to help, so you behave. Do you understand?" Hoover and Randolph looked deep into the little girl's eyes and nodded. "Good," she said. "Daddy, this is Hoover and Randolph. A murder of ten crows mobbed Hoover. His wing hurts real bad."

Harper put on the long leather gloves and walked slowly over to the big owl. "Sorry to hear you had a bad time with the crows, old man. Hoover is a fine name for a fine bird."

Hoover's eyes were half-closed, but he turned his head to watch Harper's every move. He tried to lift his clawed feet, ready to fight, but a sharp pain forced him to lay still. "Moooooaaan."

Harper carefully held the owl's legs down and reached under Hoover's wing. Hoover let out a scream, "Creeeeaaakkk!"

"I know it hurts, old man. Your wing is dislocated and you have lost some serious wing feathers." Harper's manner was so gentle that Hoover relaxed a bit. "Hoover, I am going to put your wing shoulder back where it belongs. I am sorry, but it's going to hurt." Harper pulled gently but firmly. There was a small 'pop.'

Hoover blinked three times but didn't make a sound, amazingly.

"That should be better. I will wrap it so you won't move it and reinjure it. Your feathers will grow back just fine with time and care."

"Father, what do you think of the splint I put on the roadrunner's leg?" Lucy asked. The roadrunner lay on a bed of soft hay with its leg sticking out. Lucy had wrapped orange tape firmly around a small flat stick on the injured leg. He hopped up and tried out his leg. But after a few steps he sank back down into the hay.

"It looks fine, Lucy. Your skills are improving. This roadrunner should be up and running around in a week or two," Harper said.

"His name is Roddy," Charlotte asserted.

"Glad to meet you, Roddy," Harper said. "You must be patient, if you want your leg to heal properly."

Charlotte looked closely at the roadrunner. He was looking very uncomfortable in the nest of hay. "Now, Roddy, aren't you glad Randolph picked you up and brought you to us?" Charlotte asked the roadrunner.

"I guess so," Roddy said, clacking and cooing. "But I was sure scared when that big raven picked me up out of the snow with his claws! I thought I was a goner for sure!"

"You would have been, if the coyote pack had found you," Charlotte said.

Roddy clapped his long curved beak several times. "Uh, I'm kind of hungry. Do you have any Lizards or maybe a little snake?"

"Goodness, no. But we have some veggie burgers for everyone!" Charlotte said happily.

"Kr...krrr...kruck!" Randolph asked. "A veggie what?"

"This is a veggie burger." Lucy took a round patty out of a box, broke it into bite-sized pieces, and handed several to Charlotte.

Roddy turned his head, looking with one eye then the other. He grabbed the veggie burger, flipped it in the air, caught it in his long curved beak and swallowed it whole. "Mmmmm, it's okay if you're reeeeeally hungry!"

Lucy tossed Randolph Raven a big piece of veggie burger. He carefully picked it up and swallowed. "Mmmm," he crowed, "not bad. Kr...krrr! But, well, give some to Hoover. See what he thinks."

"I had better feed Hoover," Harper said. "I don't trust his sharp beak and talons." He put on the leather gloves again.

Hoover Owl, sitting up on the hay, kept his eyes steadily on Harper and the piece of food dangling from his gloved fingers. Slowly Hoover took it in his beak, tasted, and swallowed. "Ark, ark, oooo."

Charlotte translated, "Hoover says, 'It's better than stink bugs, but he wouldn't want it every day!'"

Laughter and animal sounds erupted from the barn!

The darkness deepened. The snow made everything look like a blur of gray paint on a canvas.

Brent knew he was in serious trouble. "God, please help me!" he cried. Then he said more quietly, "I'm sorry I got angry at You, Lord. I mean before, about the fire and all."

The snow was coming down so thick, Brent didn't see the hill until he was sliding. Faster and faster he slid and tumbled, until, "Oof!"

He managed to sit up. He had hit some sort of wall. He dragged his sore body through the snow until, "Ow!" His cold hand hit a door handle. He pulled the cold metal. The door swung open. Brent fell inside along with a pile of snow. He got to his feet. His whole body was shaking with cold. He pulled the door closed behind him. At least here, he realized, he was out of the wind and snow.

It was as dark as a cave inside. As his eyes adjusted to the dimness he could just make out long benches on two sides of an aisle.

He dragged his cold feet forward. He bumped into a solid table with something on it. The object fell over with a thud. What was it? He felt across the table top. His freezing hands could just make out a shape.

"A cross!" he exclaimed, his voice barely above a whisper. "Thank You, Jesus. I was lost and now I am found. You carried me on the wings of Your wind…well, a snowy hill, to safety." He climbed up on one of the benches. He pulled his knees up to his chest, and fell asleep.

****

"Oh, Sheriff, my son has been missing since before the snow hit. I have looked everywhere!" Velina Swenson, Brent's mother, broke down in sobs. She put her hands over her face. She looked older than she really was. Her black hair had come loose from the usually neat, bun at her neck. "He's all I have."

"Now, now, Mrs. Swenson. We will find your son. We will begin looking for him as soon as we contact our search and rescue team."

****

"Yes, Sheriff. I will go now." Harper hung up the phone. "Lucy, do you know a boy named Brent Swenson? He goes to your school. I believe he is in the 6th grade like you."

"Yes, Dad. Brent's mama is a baker, well, was a baker, until the bakery burned down," Lucy answered. "What's wrong?"

"He left Mr. Benson's, where he was chopping wood yesterday and never came home."

"Oh, Daddy! Do you think he is in Heaven…like Mama?" Charlotte asked. Big tears made their way down her cheeks and spilled onto her red hoody.

"I hope not, Sweetheart." Harper took Charlotte onto his lap and put his arm around Lucy. "I'm sure he has somehow found shelter. But I know the best thing we can do is ask Jesus to help. Then I must go help look for him."

Harper closed his eyes and prayed, "Dear Lord Jesus, You know exactly where Brent is right now. And I know You love him just like You love my two girls. I pray, Lord, that You will help me or one of the other searchers to find him soon. Thank You, Lord. Amen."

"Amen," Lucy and Charlotte said.

"Daddy, can I tell the animals about Brent?" Charlotte asked. "Maybe they can help."

"Of course," he answered, as he pulled on the hood of his blue parka. "But, stay together, girls. I don't want you out in the barn alone or, God forbid, in this storm." Then he slipped his boots onto a pair of snowshoes and snapped the clamps securely.

The barn was much warmer than outside. It smelled of sweet hay.

Quickly, Charlotte went to the pile of hay, where Randolph still stayed with Hoover.

"Randolph, Brent is lost and my daddy is going to find him. Could you please help Daddy find Brent? After all, you can see so much better with your bird's eye view." She laughed and Randolph chortled at her joke.

Immediately, Randolph flew out of the barn's open loft window.

****

"Which way, Lord?" Harper talked to the Lord, just like he always talked to his best friend. The toughest time in his life had been when the love of his life was so sick. If he hadn't had Jesus, he knew he wouldn't have been able to take care of Charlotte and Lucy, during her illness and then death. Without the comfort and encouragement of Jesus, he knew he would have crumpled up and died, too. But through it all, Harper claimed the promise that Jesus would never leave him to go through the struggles of life alone. So it came natural, talking to Jesus, his Forever Friend.

Randolph Raven flew low and buzzed Harper like a small fighter plane. Harper smiled.

"That was a quick answer, Lord, thank you!" Harper laughed. "Okay, Randolph, lead the way!"

Randolph flew straight to a dark wooden building almost hidden by the snow. Randolph landed on the roof. "Awwwk!"

Harper slogged along on his snowshoes until he came to the little church.

"Randolph, did Brent find his way to Grandpa Bell's church?" Harper asked. He pulled open the door. It was dark, and very cold inside the church. He turned on his big flashlight. There were shoe tracks visible in the snow by the entrance.

"Brent, are you in here?"

There was a rustling in the front of the church. Harper hurried toward the sound. The young man was huddled on the bench, but he wasn't responding.

"Hypothermia!"

Harper worked quickly. He wrapped Brent in a wool blanket he pulled from his bag. He put his own warm hat with ear flaps on Brent's head. He worked over Brent, rubbing his back, arms and legs, warming him gradually. Finally when the boy mumbled something, Harper gave him sips of warm green tea with honey and lemon from his thermos.

Then he called the sheriff's office.

****

A deputy came to the little church and picked up Brent on a snow machine. Harper suggested that they take Brent to his house to recuperate since it was closer than the nearest hospital.

The sheriff brought Brent's mother to the Bell house in his four-wheel drive pickup.

Brent was propped up with pillows on the couch. He was wrapped in blankets like a cocoon.

"Mom!" Brent was able to smile.

"Oh my precious son!" Velina held Brent in her arms gently.

Harper stood at the kitchen door, watching the reunion.

"Mom, this is Dr. Bell. He is a veterinarian, but he is a great people doctor, too! Dr. Bell, this is my mother, Velina Swenson. She is the best baker in the whole country!"

"I'm so glad to meet you, Dr. Bell. Thank you for saving my son." Velina didn't let go of his hand after the formal hand shake.

Their eyes met for a long moment.

"I, er, would take Brent home but…well, our home over the bakery burned down and our welcome at the hotel is about over. I…"

"Daddy!" Charlotte burst into the room. "Papa, we have new babies!"

"Baby raccoons," Lucy answered. "The coyotes got the mother raccoon. We lured the babies to the barn with…"

"Veggie burgers!" They finished the sentence together, and started laughing.

"What is a veggie burger?" Brent asked.

"A veggie burger can be made with beans, corn, soy, and other veggies," Lucy explained.

"The animals eat it, but they <u>all</u> say, 'It's okay, but we wouldn't want it every day!'" laughed Charlotte.

"So you are a baker without a job, or a home?" Harper asked.

"I am," Velina answered. She shook her head sadly.

"And we are a family without a cook," Harper said, matter-of-factly.

"Hey, I cook okay for our family!" Lucy objected.

"We have lots of empty rooms upstairs!" Charlotte said excitedly.

"I think you and Brent should stay here," Harper said firmly.

"Are you sure? I can't pay you anything."

"From what I hear, your baking skills will be well worth two rooms, and well, Lucy could use a little help in the cooking department. "

"I do just fine!" Lucy said defensively.

"What is your favorite meal to cook?" Velina asked.

"Spaghetti!" Lucy said stubbornly and put her hands on her hips.

"Oh, that is my favorite!" Velina said kindly. "But I can never seem to get my sauce just right. Maybe you can teach me your secret?"

"Maybe," Lucy said. She looked into Velina's dark eyes.

"With all this talk about veggie burgers, I have to ask," Velina said, shyly. "Are you vegetarians?"

Harper burst out laughing. "No! We just buy them by the case and they are easy and sort of healthy!"

"Just wait 'til you taste mom's hamburgers," Brent said, "and apple pie for dessert!"

"Would you teach me to make apple pie?" Lucy asked quietly.

"Apple pie always tastes better when two people make it together." Velina smiled, and winked at Lucy.

Little orange and yellow wild flowers announced spring. Meadowlarks and mocking birds sang their arrival. Harper and Brent planted corn. Velina, Charlotte, and Lucy, planted squash, beets, and carrots.

One day, Harper brought home a grocery bag full of little packets.

"What is this?" Velina asked.

"Flower seeds, so you can decorate the yard, like you have decorated our home, dear lady," Harper said. His gray eyes met her deep-brown eyes. Their gaze held for a long moment.

Velina looked away, but her cheeks were a bright pink. "I don't know what you are talking about, Harper Bell," she said with a nervous laugh.

"You have brought color and joy not only into our home, but into my heart, as well." He touched her hand gently.

****

Hoover and Maizy Owl watched over two almost-white eggs in their big stick nest.

Randolph had met a very pretty raven named Rita. They danced in the air and he sang love songs to her.

Roddy Roadrunner was running through the young cornstalks. His leg was as good as new. He heard rustling in the next row. He stopped. The rustling stopped.

"Friend or foe?" Roddy asked.

"Foe or friend?" came the answer.

Roddy crouched low and step-by-step crossed into the next corn row.

"Boooooo!"

Roddy spun around. There was the loveliest lady roadrunner Roddy had ever seen!

****

Two lame horses, an elderly goat, and a pregnant sheep were in the barn, as well as various dogs and cats in pens waiting for Harper's expert doctoring. The baby raccoons had grown into teenagers and would soon move into the woods to be independent.

Harper and Velina were getting married on Saturday at the little brown church. Charlotte and Lucy had decorated the church with bouquets of purple, orange, and white wild flowers. Everyone from the village came to the wedding and brought food for a banquet after the wedding.

Brent joked, "Mom, now you are Vel Bell!"

Harper ruffled Brent's hair. "And you can be Brent Bell, if you want to be."

"That sounds just fine to me." Brent hugged Harper. "Does that mean I can call you Dad?"

"I wouldn't have it any other way!"

And if you were very observant, you could see that there were many guests, other than just people, at the wedding!

Hello, dear reader.
I am a great horned owl named Hoover.
Randolph Raven, is a real mover.
We live on the great windy plains.
This story is about change:
Dark to light, death to life, fear to hope.
Some understand animals in prose.
Charlotte is one of those.
Annabel Montgomery, inspires with a brush.
Ruth and Larry Bradford write in the hush.

Great Horned Owl surveys all without fail.
Cocky raven keeps watch from porch rail.
Roadrunner paces to no avail.
Ruth & Larry Bradford tell this tale
(Photos taken of our winged visitors to our yard in in New Mexico)

Larry and Ruth Bradford are retired elementary school teachers.
They have taught in Oregon, Alaska, New Mexico, and The Philippines.
They now live in New Mexico. Ruth does the writing,
but Larry's sense of humor and creative ideas bring the stories alive.

Annabel Montgomery was raised on a horse farm in New Mexico.
She and her husband, Johnny, moved to the mountains in 2003.
She didn't begin painting until 2017.
She is blessed by this new gift God has given her,
and loves blessing others.

Other Books By The Authors

The Perfect Gift & The Perfect Sacrifice
(Historical Fiction about Jesus)
I Kissed The Fish (Middle
grade fiction in Alaska)
The Little Wood Hauler (Historical
Fiction in Yukon, Canada)
Kerry, Kitty, & The War (Historical
Fiction WWII in Ireland)
The Kid Whisperer (Biographical sketch
of Lorraine Lamar in the Philippines)

CPSIA information can be obtained
at www.ICGtesting.com
Printed in the USA
BVHW021202181019
561474BV00003B/58/P